This book belongs to:

_____

_____

_____

For Henry

First published 1996 by Walker Books Ltd
87 Vauxhall Walk, London SE11 5HJ

This edition published 2014

2 4 6 8 10 9 7 5 3 1

© 1996 Sue Hendra

The right of Sue Hendra to be identified as author/illustrator of this work
has been asserted by her in accordance with the Copyright,
Designs and Patents Act 1988

This book has been typeset in Times Educational

Printed in China

British Library Cataloguing in Publication Data:
a catalogue record for this book is available from the British Library

ISBN 978-1-4063-5875-9

www.walker.co.uk

Oliver's Wood

Sue Hendra

WALKER BOOKS
AND SUBSIDIARIES
LONDON • BOSTON • SYDNEY • AUCKLAND

When night falls and the moon and the twinkly stars come out, Oliver wakes up in his wood. "Tu-whit-tu-whoo!" he calls.

The spiky hedgehogs
and the stripy badgers
wake up in the wood, too.
Snuffle, snuffle.

They are Oliver's friends.

So are the batty bats.
Oliver likes to fly around
with them in the wood.
Whizz, whizz.

Oliver and his friends
play all night long.
Then, when the moon
and the twinkly stars
grow dim, they go
to sleep.

One night, Oliver stayed
up late. He saw the moon
and the twinkly stars
grow dim …

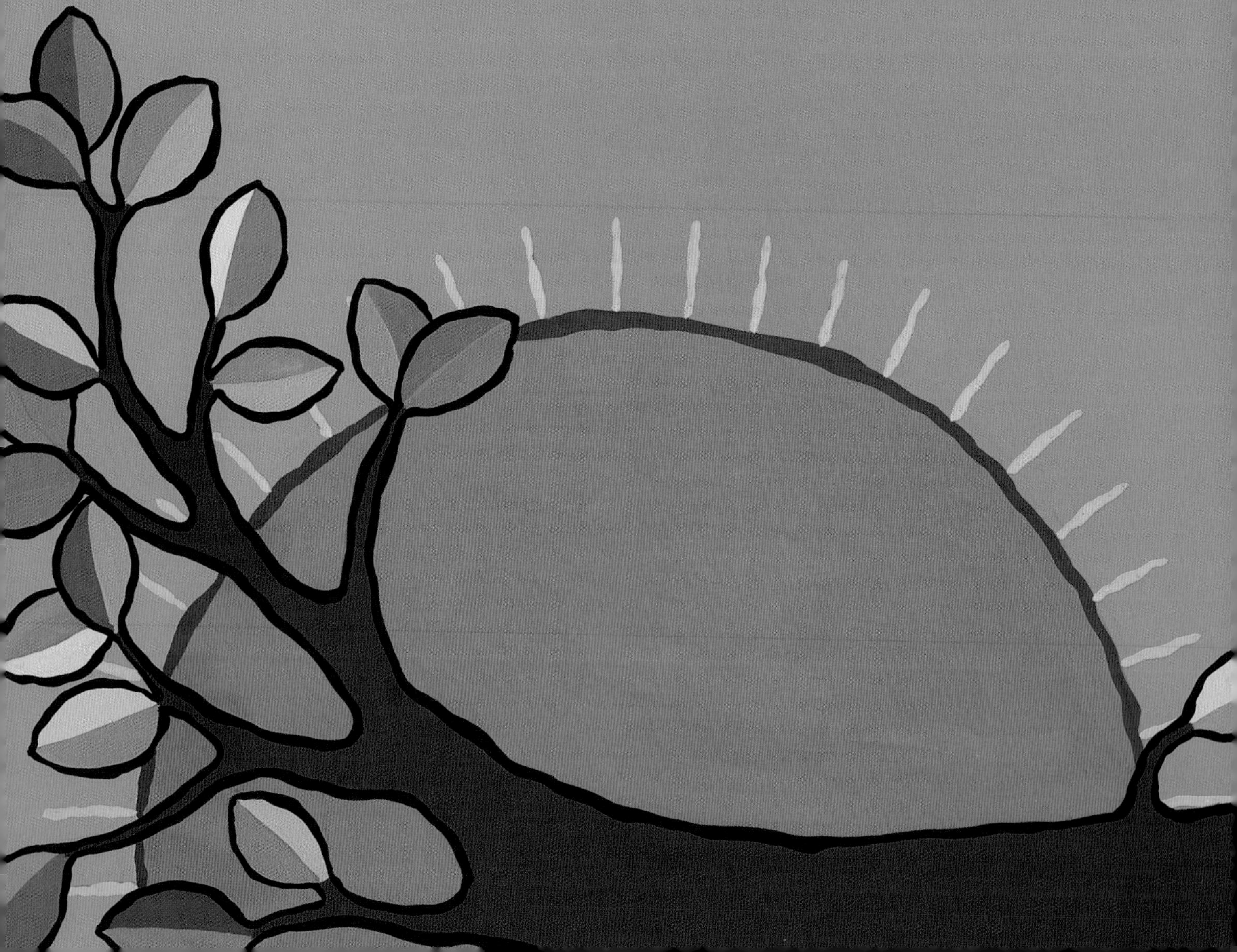

and then he saw something
he had never seen before.
The big, round, warm,
orange sun!

Oliver was very excited. He went to tell the spiky hedgehogs and the stripy badgers, but instead there were rabbits and squirrels.

Hippety-hop, went the rabbits. Scitter-scatter, went the squirrels. They didn't talk to Oliver.

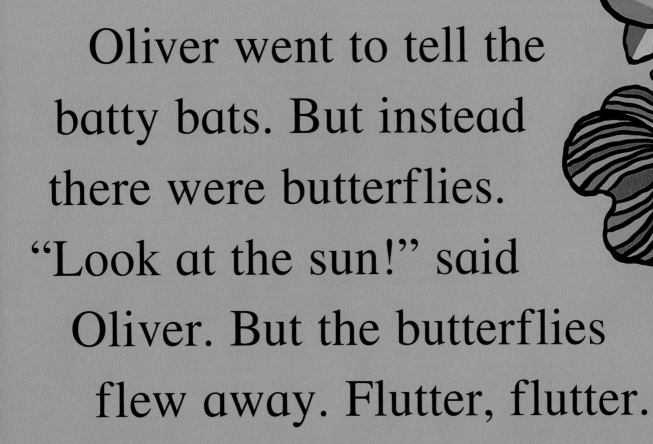

Oliver went to tell the batty bats. But instead there were butterflies. "Look at the sun!" said Oliver. But the butterflies flew away. Flutter, flutter.

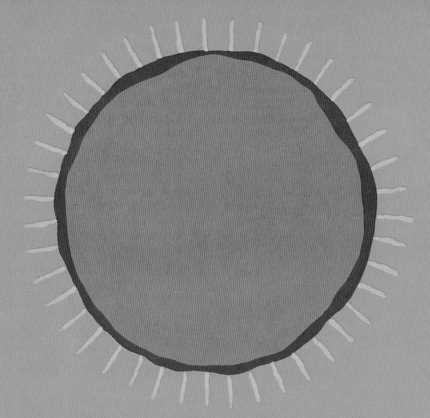

Oliver felt very lonely.
He flew back to his branch.

He wished he could tell
someone about the sun.

Oliver lay down on
his branch and slept.

Night fell and Oliver's friends
came out to play in the wood.
"Wake up, lazybones!"
they shouted.

When Oliver opened his
eyes and saw all his friends,
he felt very happy.
"Guess what," he called,
"I saw the big, round,
warm, orange sun!"

"Wow!" said the
prickly hedgehogs
and the stripy badgers.
"Whee!" said the batty bats.
"Tu-whit-tu-whoo!"
hooted Oliver.